The Official
ONE AND ONLY
Imperial Wizard Approved

HALL OF FAME GUIDEBOOK

Written by Brendan Behan Pullen

Illustrated by Salvadore Dali Pullen

George Spain, Editor in Chief

ISBN 978-1-62880-115-6

First edition, January 2017

Images pages viii, 2 ,16, 17, 18, 19, 20, 21, 22, 24, 28, 38 found in *Seeing the Insane*, by Sander L. Gilman, Ph.D., 1982, John Wiley & Sons, New York, NY. Covered by Copyright Act of 1976, Sec. 103: This Act does not provide copyright protection for any work that goes into the public domain before January 1, 1978.

Printed in the United States of America on acid free paper.

APPRECIATION

This guidebook is partially funded with a grant from the National Association For The Development And Preservation Of Halls Of Fame. NAFTDAPOHOF is dedicated to the belief that everyone should have a Hall of Fame irrespective of sex, race, religion, national origin, height, sexual orientation, right or left side of brain dominance or waist size.

Thanks is also due the following people who have purchased advertisements* included in the guidebook:

Bo Bo Ledgetter's Lumber Yards
*Delightful Suthun Madnesses XIII**
Dr. Kinky Sexmund
Dr. Funk's Trusty Triboelectric Truss
Flem Snopes Ten Foot Wooden Safety Matches
Hog Higgin's Service Stations
Hoods and Robes by Kuties
Katzenberger's Klancraft Kross Kumpany, Inc.
Keep Kovers Klean Detergent
"Mule Man" McInity, Inc.
Nathan Bedford Forrest White Bed Sheets Manufacturing Co., Inc.
One Ear's Stickers
Sir Arthur "Doony Gene" Pendragon's Armory, Inc.
The Peeky Poo Nudist Camp

*All products except *Delightful Suthun Madnesses XIII* which we included only because they paid for an ad and not because we wanted to can be ordered through KKK National Headquarters.

NATHAN
BEDFORD
FORREST
WHITE BEDSHEETS
MANUFACTURING
COMPANY, INC.

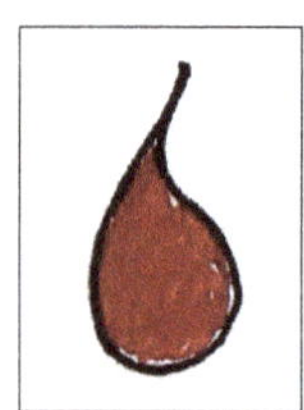

THE
KU KLUX KLAN

 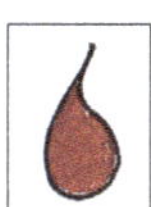

HALL OF FAME

IS CONSTANTLY TOURING AMERICA!

Watch for this pure white semi trailer
with the logo of
General Nathan Bedford Forrest.
It may be in your town soon.

In it you will learn the true and glorious
history of the Klan!
See here-to-fore unpublished photographs of great Ku Kluxxers.
Read inspiring quotations and stories.
Learn how to make your own cross at home.

Now, many, many other
wondrous Klan secrets
Will Be Revealed!

This Imperial Wizard approved guidebook, yours at nominal cost, is a
must when you and your family tour the

K K K HALL OF FAME!

K.K.K. Hall of Fame.

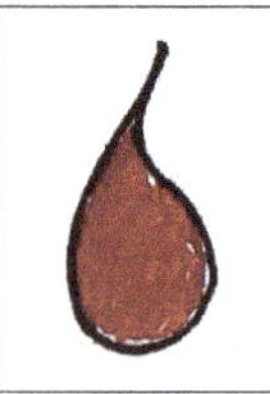

GENERAL NATHAN BEDFORD FORREST

Brendan Behan Pullen

Salvadore Dali Pullen

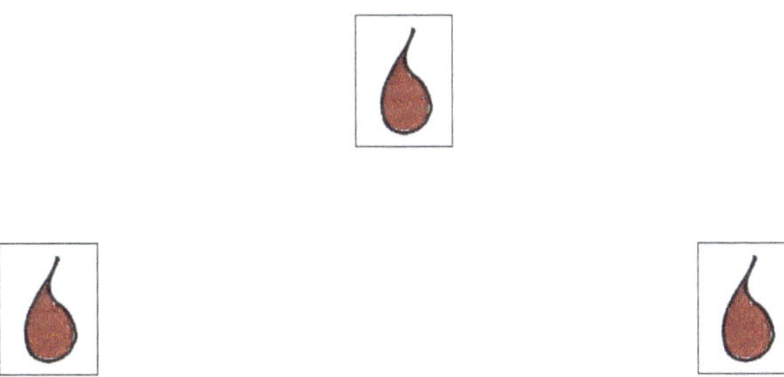

"Beware, that stern lean-man who possesseth truth,
He may burneth thee upon yon stake, forsooth!
Pray, tweaketh his long nose whenever thou it can,
For it helpeth him recall, that he is but a man."

—St. Joebobius Tweakius

"If, after I depart this vale, you ever remember me and have
thought to please my ghost, forgive some sinner and wink your
eye at some homely girl."

—H.L. Mencken

Dedicated to the Memories
of two
Great Nose Tweakers

ST. JOEBOBIUS TWEAKIUS
AND
H. L. MENCKEN

St. Joebobius Tweakius
legendary 5th century
Irish monk, who originated
nose-pinching for dealing
with pompous born-again
Druids

H.L. Mencken
a sho'nuff 20th century
journalist, whose pen
pinched the priggish noses
of the Booboisie until
they cried, "Uncle."

"magna est veritas et praevalebit"
"truth will out, like jersey cream rising"

CONTENTS

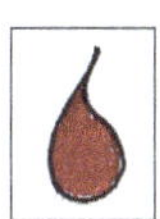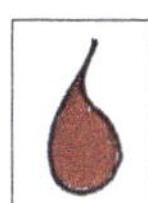

AKIA! Greetings! AKAK?

Fellow Klansmen  Klansmen to Be

 WELCOME TO THE KU KLUX KLAN HALL OF FAME

We know your tour will be Pleasant and Informative. Too long, the commiepinkoliberals and egghead news reporters have profaned the Noble History of our Beloved Klan. Too long, have we been maligned as ignorant, paranoid, bigoted, mean, humorless, ugly-acting white trash. Too long, have we kept silent in proclaiming the Klan's Legacy of Exemplary Courage, Pure Chivalrous Purpose, and Christian Good Works!

Now, through the Generosity of the Reknown Katzenberger Family and their Public Spirited Coorporation [sic], Nathan Bedford Forrest White Bed Sheets Manufacturing Company, Incorporated, you will learn how and what the Klan contributes to the American Way of Life. Now, through actual photographs and stories of Great Klan Leaders, you will be Blest and Inspired. Now, you will be able to sleep better at night, knowing We Are Here!

As long as Good People, such as You, give us Moral Support, Pay Membership Dues and Buy Katzenberger Products the Klan will remain— Healthy, Wealthy and Wise!

Your friend—

 *The Imperial Wizard* 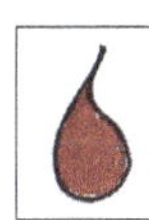

HISTORICAL BEGINNINGS

K. K. Katzenberger III

 that the Klan was started as a social club in Pulaski, Tennessee, in December, 1865 by six young ex-Confederates. Not so! The truth of the Klan's origin is now revealed for the first time. It did indeed begin in 1865, but the location was Hartford, Connecticut and it was founded by this man, K. K. Katzenberger III. "Triple K.", as he was known by intimates, was a shrewd carpetbagger and manufacturer of white bed sheets. He sensed that there were huge profits to be made in a "reconstructed" South if he could only come up with an original marketing idea. The rest is history.

*In 1915, Katzenberger Manu. Co. changed its name to Nathan Bedford Forrest White Bed Sheet Manu. Co., Inc. In this same year there was a Klan resurgence.

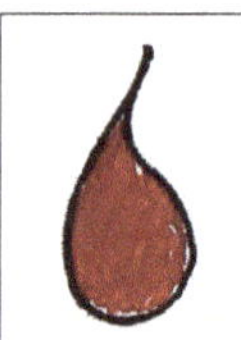

ORIGIN OF THE NAME
KU KLUX KLAN

Other than manufacturing his white bed sheets and making money, K.K. Katzenberger III had two other loves in his carpetbagging heart, Egyptology and transvestism. Only a few old and trusted servants knew of "Triple K's" late night glides and twirls through his mansion dressed in a flowing sheet. Gliding from room to room his idea for a secret men's society, dressed in Katzenberger sheets, flowed toward its ultimate inspiration. He would name and develop the new society after a secret Egyptian organization which was founded in 1421 B.C. during the Tuthmosis IV dynasty. Dedicated to gay rights the society's name in hieroglyphics was:

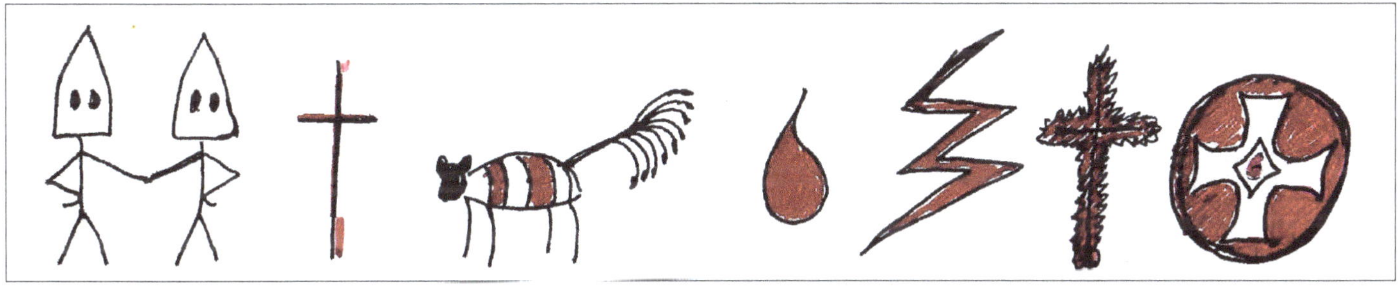

The literal translation into English left much to be desired: *Sissy KooKoo Klutz-Men*

"Triple K" was no fool. He realized that the name of the new society needed dressing up as much as he needed to dress its members in Katzenberger sheets. He took one more flow through the mansion and, as the blood flowed through his brain, the name for his secret society became:

KU KLUX KLAN

HOW TO MAKE YOUR

Follow These Easy Steps:

1. Get two (2) pieces of wood and lay one across the other like this

2. Get some nails and hammer them in here

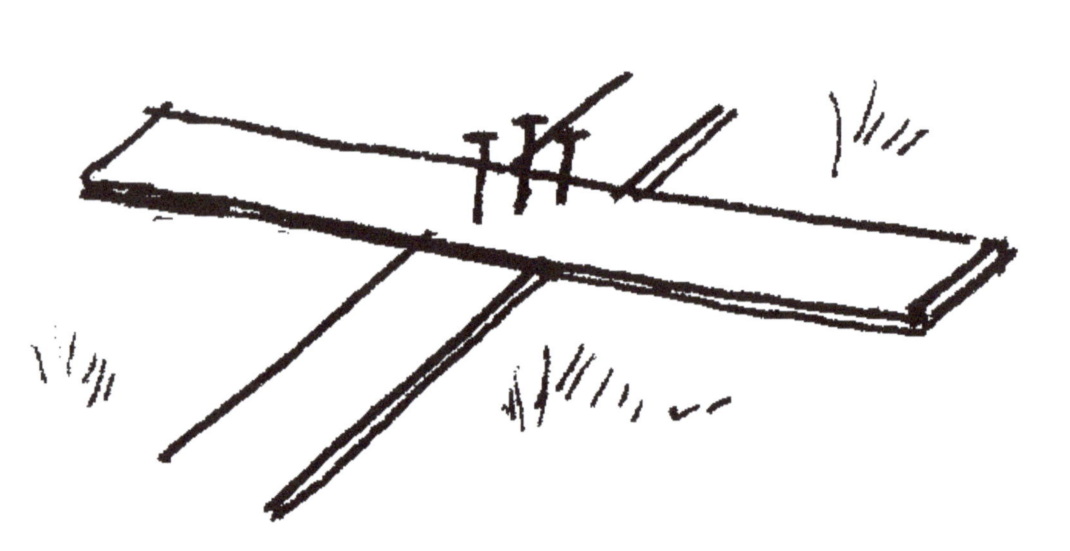

OWN CROSS AT HOME

3. Dig a hole in the ground like this

4. Put cross in hole in K.K.K. officially approved position:

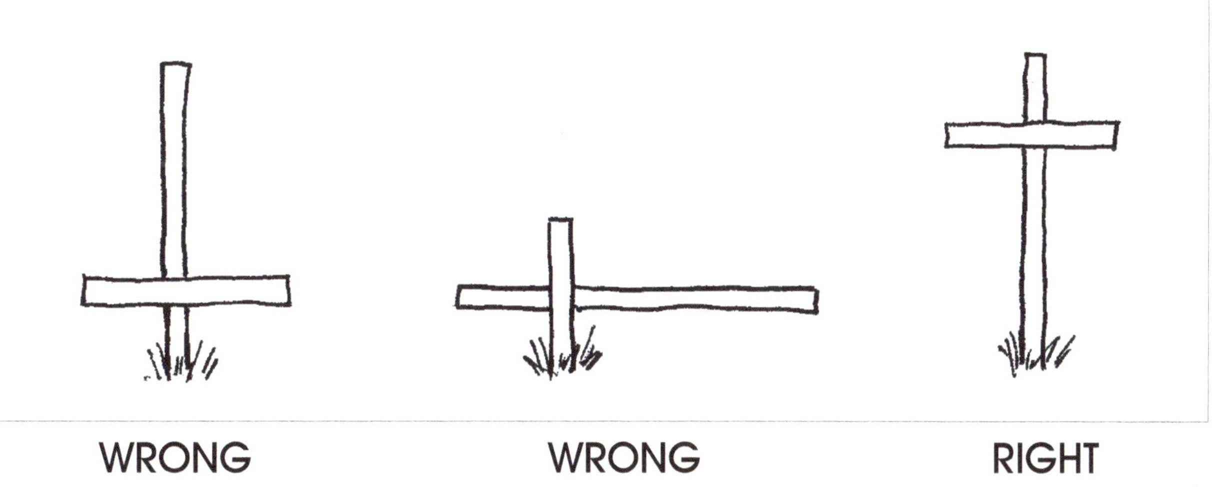

3 or 4. Wrap the cross
in gunnysacks
and tie them on
with heavy twine
like this

4 or 5. Get you some used
crank-case oil and gas*
and pour it all over
the cross
like this.

6. Now, previous step 4 is step 6, which is putting your ready-to-burn cross back into the hole you dug.

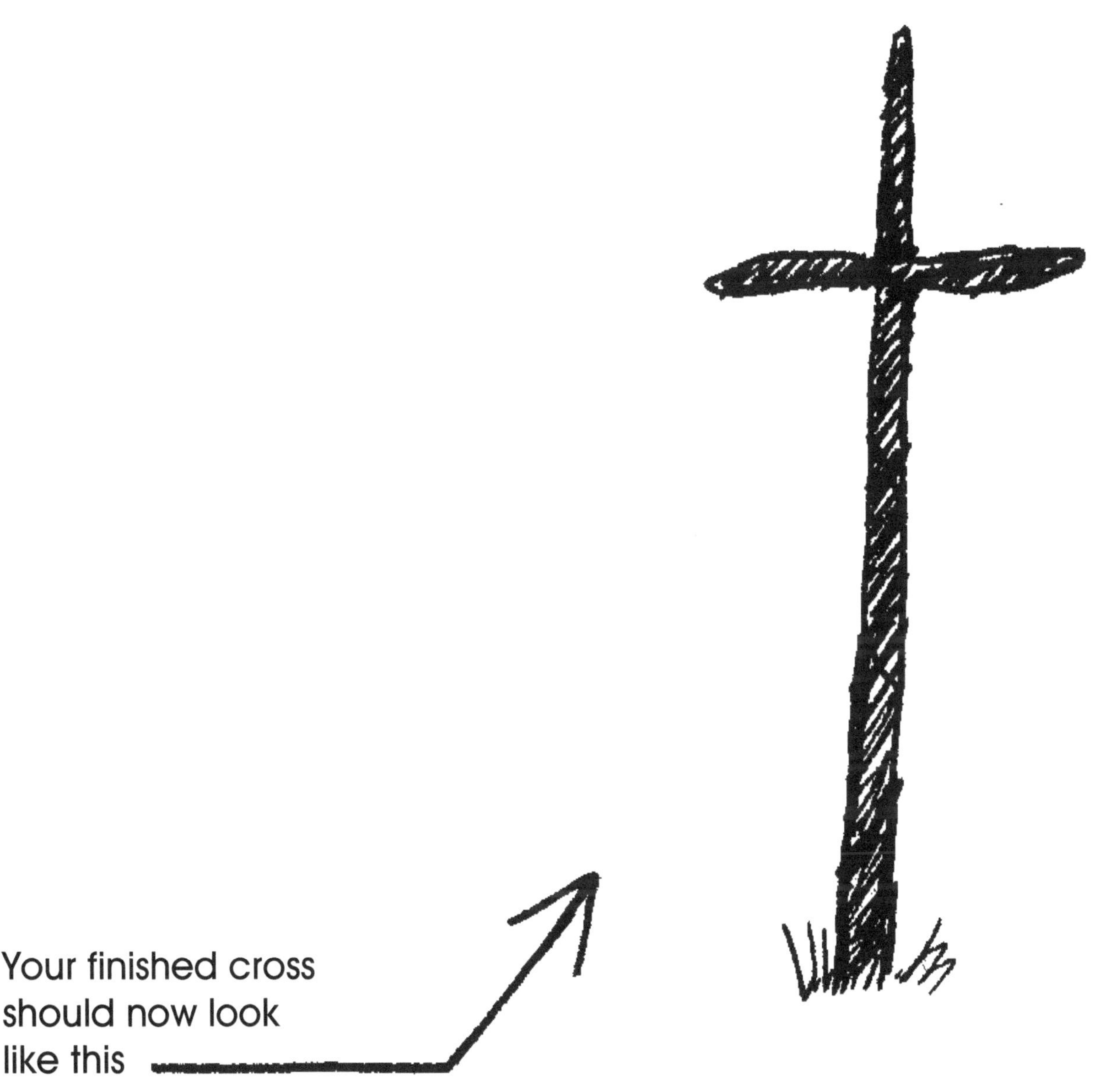

Your finished cross should now look like this

Ain't she a beauty!

*use 5 pounds of oil and ½ gallon of gasoline for every foot of cross.

K.K.K. APPROVED SAFE

Flamethrower

Special KKK
Electronic Cross Lighter

10' Wooden
Safety Match

Asbestos Hood,
Robe and Gloves

WAYS TO LIGHT A CROSS

Bow and Arrow*

A Really Fast
Klansman

Gunpowder Trail

Use a Klutz

*Caution: Be sure no Klansmen are on the far side of the cross.

WARNING!!!

CROSS BURNING
MAY BE HAZARDOUS
TO YOUR HEALTH

HOW NOT TO LIGHT A CROSS

HISTORICAL IMAGES: PHOTOGRAPHS, LITHOGRAPHS, PORTRAITS, AND MORE

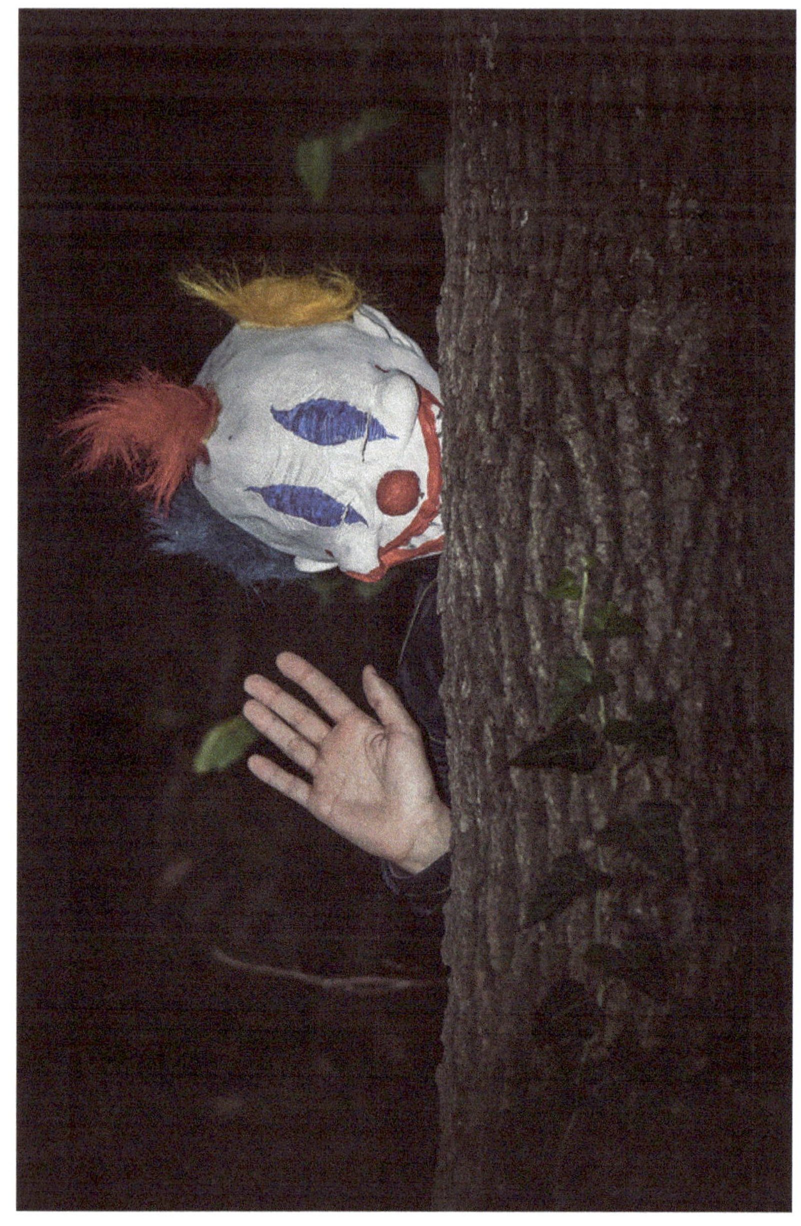

 is flooded with requests for photographs of our beloved Imperial Wizard, without his robe and hood on. Well here he is, the indomitable Fleetwood "The Clown" Goering.

AN EXTREMELY RARE photograph of the infamous Remus X. During his entire 10 years in the Klan no one ever saw him without his robe and hood. Remus X held many leadership positions, from Klockard to Genil, and is here shown dressed as a Night-Hawk. While fellow Klansmen sometimes wondered why he never relaxed, and got comfortable, without all his paraphernalia on, they marked it up to his extreme dedication to the cause (though some still thought he was a tad weird).

He explained his dark hands were the result of his profession, walnut gathering and hulling. Suspicion about his true identity did not arise until the summer of 1982 when, at a Klavern picnic, he adamantly refused to eat watermelon and fried chicken. Immediately after the picnic he disappeared. Soon afterward, he appeared on Saturday Night Live, still robed and hooded, and there revealed that Remus X was none other than a FBI agent and, to make matters worse, was black!

THE REVEREND WHIP LA GREE, first Grand Kludd and unknown biblical scholar, praying that God will smite all Klan enemies with locusts, ringworm, plaque, athlete's foot, high taxes, boils and hernias. Reverend La Gree is noted for his continuing best seller, "How God Messed Up When He Got All Wore Down." In this definitive study Reverend La Gree brilliantly shows how God got fatigued by the sixth day of creation and blundered terribly on his first try at making man. Then, with flawless logic, he proves that on the afternoon of the seventh day, following a good night's sleep, God successfully achieved perfection by making White Anglo-Saxon Protestants.

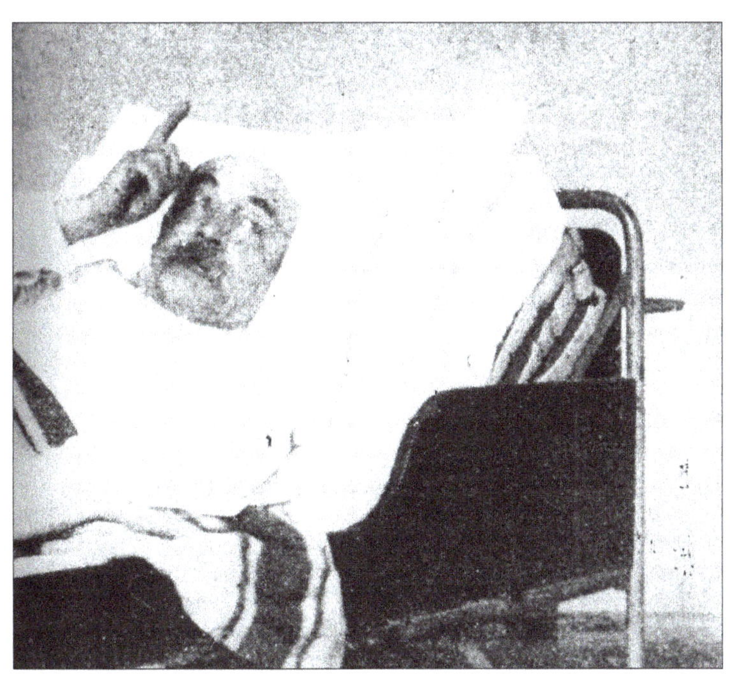

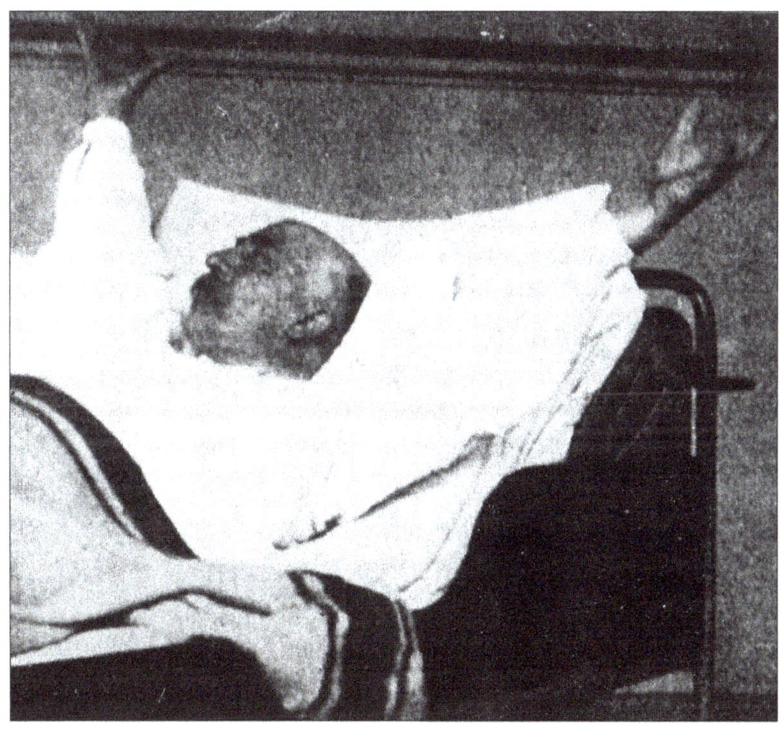

THIS IS NONE OTHER than the reknown Grand Cyclops, Colonel Beauregard Q. Calhoun. "The Colonel," as he was fondly known, stayed in his bed for the last twenty-seven years of his life in protest of the 1954 Supreme Court ruling on Brown vs. Board of Education which resulted in school integration. The photo on the top shows "The Colonel" talking ugly to Federal Marshals who are attempting to get him to move his bed from blocking the front door of a school. On the bottom we see "The Colonel" surrendering to the Federal Marshals.

MISS ROSEBUD PEEVY was still fit to be tied when this picture was made. She had just stormed out of a tent revival where the minister had condemned her with Proverbs xix,5:

"A false witness shall not be unpunished, and he that speaketh lies shall not escape."

Rosebud, who was no shrinking violet, shouted back:

*"Reverend Love, Ah nuvuh said you was no membuh of the Ku Klux Klan, awl Ah eva said was that you certainly ah a wizard unduh tha sheet!"**

Reverend Love was later tarred and feathered while Rosebud was chosen Miss Klan Sweetheart of 1924.

*This quotation weren't right in the section on "Wizard Under the Sheet Disorder" in *Delightful Southern Madnesses XIII*. Do not trust that book.

Noted **Klan** bumper-sticker designer, Vincent "One Ear" Mullins. One ear's specialty is clever poetical couplets which educate and warn true Americans of the evil threats pervading our nation. Good examples are the following which you have surely seen on numerous bumpers:

THIS IS A SECRET LITHOGRAPH of the entire board of directors of Katzenberger Klankraft Kross Kumpany, Inc.

It was made by a Klansman disguised as a German shepherd guard dog. Klankraft was the original manufacturer of the prefabricated cross which is now available in many hardware stores. The only surviving board member is Claude "Crazy Eyes" Hess (circled in red) who has proclaimed for the last 39 years that he is a leaf of prime burley tobacco.

AN EARLY PHOTOGRAPH of six new Klan members attempting to learn the Klan's secret salute. The two seated in front and one standing on the right were eventually kicked out because of chronic self abuse and giggling at Klan meetings.

FROM ITS BEGINNING the Klan has drawn to its membership many profound thinkers and philosophers. None have more fearlessly attacked the great questions of morality, life and death than the Great Klockard, Earl Dee Brightwater. His book *Earl Dee's Words of Wisdom and Guidance* has now become a standard text for the Klan Youth Corps. Monthly Klavern meetings include group recitations of such profound Earl Dee saying* as:

"A bird in the hand is dead!"

"Since man is immortal his meat bill will be astronomical!"

"The ultimate answer lies within the heart of all of us. The answer is twelve!"

"Belief in an afterlife requires that one is always prepared with an extra change of underwear!"

"Sex is nobody else's business except the three people involved."

*Charges of plagiarism and complete absence of humor have been filed against Earl Dee by the noted Brooklyn Freudian soothsayer Woody Allen who says of Earl Dee, "He does not make the Ha Ha."

THIS IS THE ONLY known photograph of the legendary Jimbo "Bighead" Hutte, who made his place in history by designing the Klan hood.

OLD "TRIPLE K'S" perverted sense of humor shines through in this extremely rare 1870 etching. In his study of the origins of ancient words "Triple K" discovered that the word dragon came from the Greek word *drakon*, which was derived from a remote verb meaning "to look at" and "to flash."

Until "Triple K's" death, when it was removed from the swearing-in ceremony, new Grand Dragons were required "to flash" themselves before the entire assembly of Klansmen.

THIS PATHETIC SOUL is a member of the K.K.

America's sexual revolution left its mark on the Klan. In the 1960s, there sprang up a splinter group called the "Klan Kuties." They wear garishly colored, sequined robes and see-through hoods which display their crowns, stylish hairdos, earrings, eye makeup and beauty spots. Under their robes they are buck-naked.

 it is not unusual to find Ku Kluxers, such as these two gentlemen, who like to dress up like knights and go around talking in old-timey ways about chivalry, King Arthur and such like. Only Klansmen of considerable wealth can afford the armor, weaponry, horses, horse trailers, Old English speech lessons, and medical treatment for lance wounds. The basis for their beliefs and practices is taken from the 1868 revision of the Klan's original prescript which states:

"This is an institution of Chivalry, Humanity, Mercy, and Patriotism; embodying in its genius and principles all that is chivalric in conduct, noble in sentiment, generous in manhood, and patriotic in purpose..."

While Klansmen who are really into King Arthur and chivalry tend to be a tad eccentric, they are generally more enjoyable to be around as they talk nicer and are not prone to run around at night-time acting ugly.

that truly Great American, Senator Joe "Thumbscrew" McKlanthy, undoubtedly the man most feared by the Kremlin. His total commitment to catching commies was shown in 1950 when he turned his grandmother, parents, younger sister, and several cousins over for investigation to the House Un-American Activities Committee. However, it was in 1979 that he made his lasting mark on our nation's history. That was the year he saved America! That was the year he led the Klan's boycott on Girl Scout Cookies.

You will readily recall the night he appeared on prime-time, national television and announced that he had in his possession secret documents* which undeniably proved that the commies had successfully infiltrated and were now in control of the sale of Girl Scout Cookies. Who of us can forget the horror felt when he further revealed that cookie sale money was being channeled to Castro for the singularly evil purpose of financing a Cuban invasion of Atlantic City? Of course these revelations were strongly denied by the C.I.A., Secretary of State, President, and the Girl Scouts of America. But we know the truth, and the ultimate proof is incontestable—because Castro knew the Klan was on to him, there was no invasion of Atlantic City.

*These documents were obtained by the Klan Bureau of Investigation (K.B.I.) from a double agent whose code name was KaKa (Klan Agent-Cuban Agent).

"Knock Kneed" is present Board Chairman of Nathan Bedford Forrest White Bed Sheet Manufacturing Company, Incorporated. When the Board is faced with particularly difficult N.B.F.W.B.S.M.C., Inc., and K.K.K. marketing strategies, it is not unusual for "Knock Kneed" to seek visionary guidance by going into the Katzenberger glide.

*The Katzenberger Glide should not be confused with "Walks to a Different Drummer Disorder" in that piece of trash *Delightful Suthun Madnesses XIII*.

KU KLUX KLAN
SECRET* HANDSHAKE

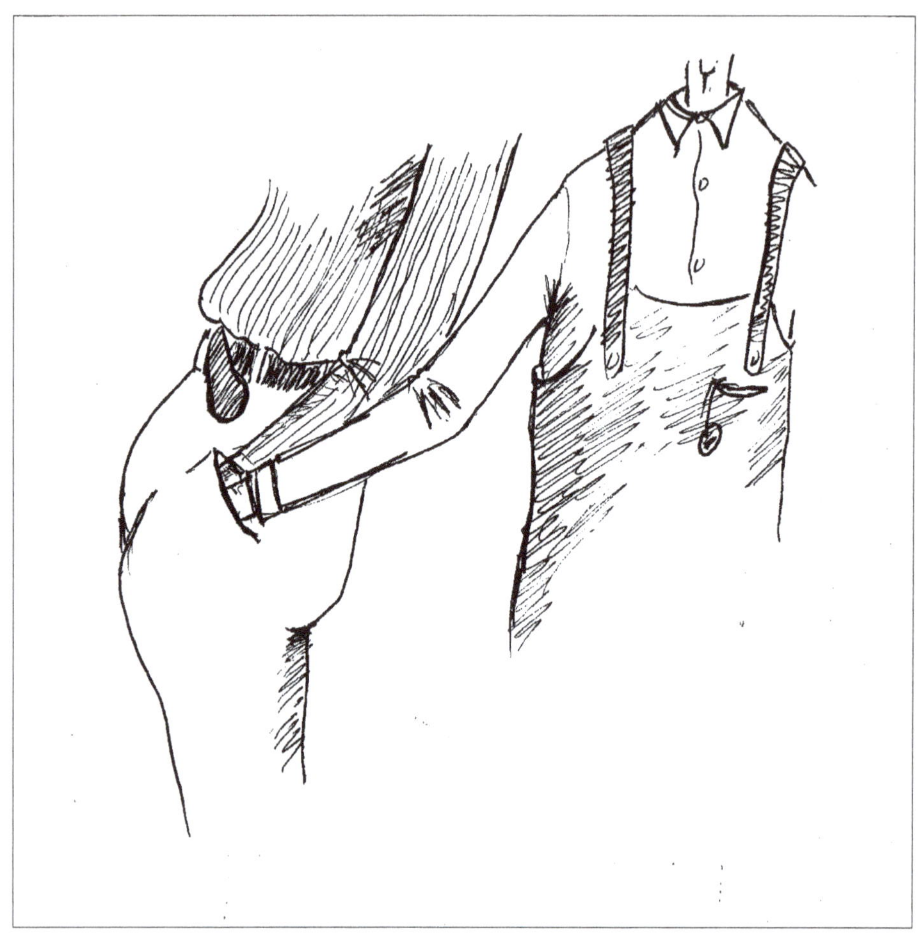

*The secret handshake is so secret we can only show here how to best disguise your greeting so no observer will be suspicious, or notice anything out of the ordinary.

Appreciation is extended to the two fine gentlemen who posed for this illustration, C.T. and B.J.

Favorite K.K.K. Limericks

by
Dylan "Welsh" Potts
Klan Poet Laureate

The Imperial Wizard named Joe Pete,
Is more than a little offbeat,
   He belongs to the Klan,
   Just so he can
Go buck-naked under his sheet.

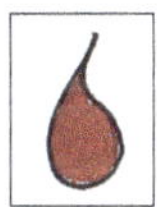 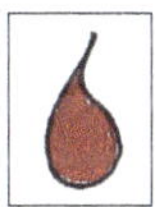 

The preacher of the Klan is a Kludd,
He believes God shaped man from the mud,
   And that W.A.S.P.s were made better,
   After an error,
Which turned the first batch into a dud.

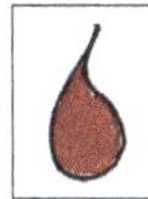 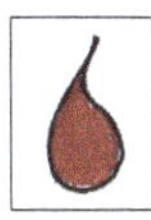 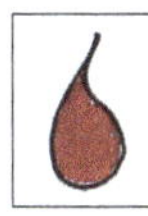

There was a Klan woman named Gertie,
Who was mean because she was dirty,
   But when she was clean,
   She wasn't so mean,
In fact, I thought Gertie was purty.

The Ku Klux Klan, White Man's Burden Blues

I work like hell to give a fright,
I run around a lot at night,
I get no respect in the news,
Marchin's made holes in all my shoes.

REFRAIN:
I buy my sheets and pay my dues,
I wear a pair of worn-out shoes,
I got the KKK, White Man's Burden Blues.

A Klansman's life is full of shocks,
Folks hit on you with sticks and rocks,
My hands are burnt, my back's a loss,
Ruptured myself liftin' a cross.
(Refrain)

My wife's sulled up, she's always mad,
Treats me sumpin' terrible bad,
Won't wash my sheets, or shine my shoes,
Talks ugly 'bout the Wizard's dues.
(Refrain)

My kid is big on Civil Rights,
He dances ballet in flesh-toned tights,
Wears a ring in his left ear lobe
And dresses in a sequined robe.
(Refrain)

I'm plumb wore down, I've been abused.
Hot Damn! The soles come off my shoes.
Unless, next year, the Klan improves,
They'll suck air, 'fore I'll pay dues.
(Refrain)

It ain't fittin' to live this way.
If things don't change, then I just may,
Go sell my sheets and take my dues,
And buy myself some brand new shoes.
(Refrain)

EPILOGUE
I joined a new group, just this year,
They've rernt my brand new shoes, I fear.
They march a lot and charge a fee,
They're named: N. Double A. C. P.
I buy no sheets, but still pay dues,
I wear a pari of worn-out shoes,
I got the WORN-OUT SHOES,
PORE MAN'S BURDEN BLUES.

Written by the Ever Popular
Klan Klode Lyricist—
Unclebrother Littlegeorge

This advertisement bought and paid for by *Delightful Suthun Madnesses XIII*.
Do not buy this book. It has not been endorsed by the KKK.
"The author and artist deserve what they get!"—KKK.

KKK Authorized and Approved

ADVERTISEMENTS

Klan clothing
Therapists
Bumper stickers,
Etc.
Etc.
Etc.
Etc.

Does Your Mule Need Fixin'?
If So, Bring It To Me
"MULE MAN" MCINITY, INC.*
I'll Fix It, Or Pay For Its Trip To The Glue Factory
*subsidiary of K.K. Katzenberger Konglomerate, Inc.

PYROMANIA

A common symptom of "burn out" occurring in Klanaholics

- Are fellow Klansmen no longer inviting you to cross burnings?
- Have you developed a fetish about matches or cigarette lighters, and carry them in your pants pocket so you can sensually stroke them?
- Are you obsessively fantasizing big burning crosses and committing the sin of Onan?
- Do you get high when you smell smoke?
- When you see something on fire, do big conveys of quail flush inside your head?

If you answer one of the above with a "yes," you are probably developing a touch of PYROMANIA!

Two yesses to any of those questions means you are now a full blown PYROMANIAC!

With professional treatment you can be helped!

Call the National Headquarters today and get an appointment to see

Dr. Kinky Sexmund, G.S., H.S., B.A., M.A., Ph.D., K.K.K., Inc.*

Dr. Kinky has received the Imperial Wizard stamp of approval for his specialized treatment of PYROMANIA.

*subsidiary of K.K. Katzenberger Konglomerate, Inc.

Having a Cross Burning?
Do you frequently have trouble getting your cross to burn?
Could you be using cheap quality cross starting fuel?
Then you need

HOG HIGGIN'S USED CRANK-CASE OIL!

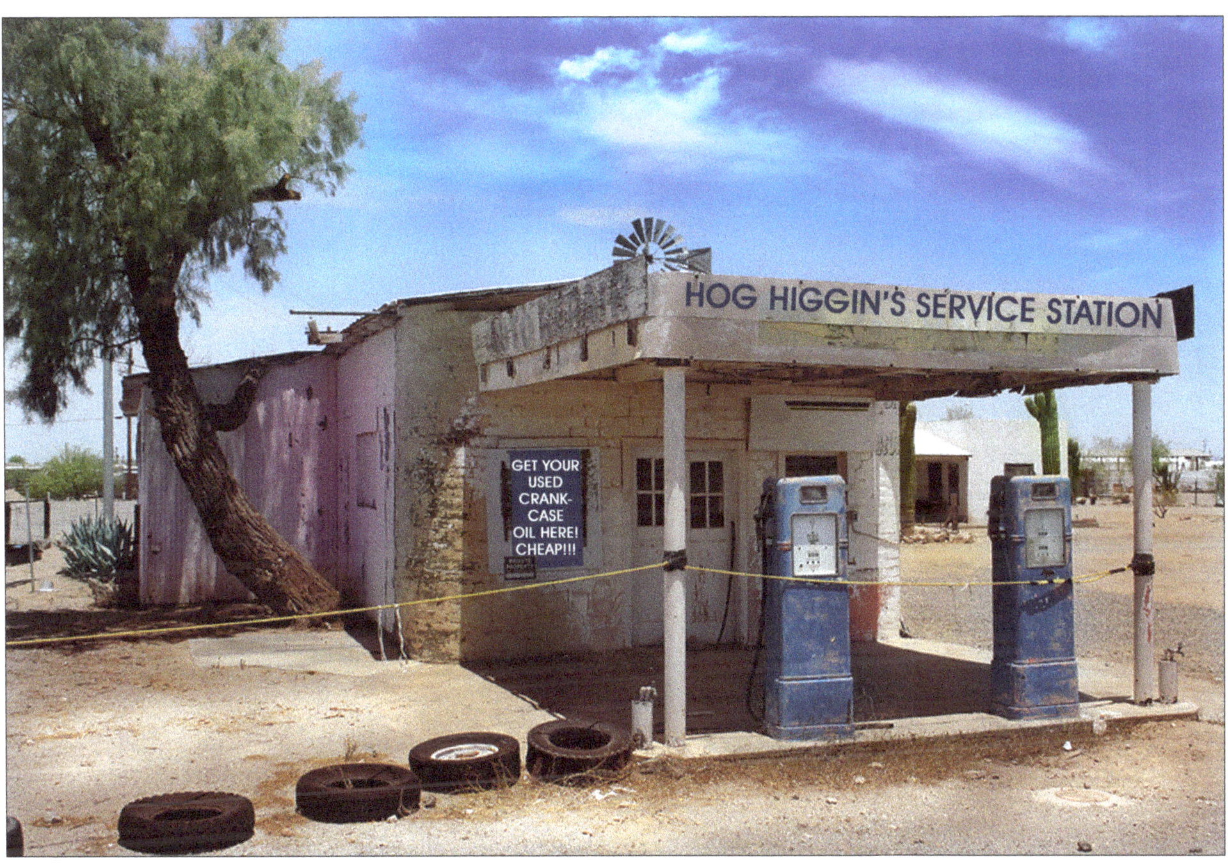

Go today to your nearest Hog Higgin's Service Station, Inc.*
Identify yourself with the secret handshake and you will receive
your used crank-case oil at the low, low KKK price, plus Hog's
special warranty which assures:

"Your cross will burn to a crisp!"

*subsidiary of K.K. Katzenberger Konglomerate, Inc.

Have you got a busted gut
from trying to lift a heavy cross?
Hernias, along with burns, are the most frequent
occupational injuries suffered by Ku Kluxers.
If your guts are ruptured, get Dr. Funk's trusty

TRIBOELECTRIC TRUSS, INC.*

with the bright red Klan symbol.

*subsidiary of K.K. Katzenberger Konglomerate, Inc.

KATZENBERGER'S KLANCRAFT KROSS KOMPANY, INC.*

Inventor and Sole Distributor of the Prefabricated Cross

KEEP KOVERS KLEAN DETERGENT, INC.*

FLEM SNOOPE'S TEN FOOT WOODEN SAFETY MATCHES, INC.*

"ONE EARS" STICKERS, INC.*

Bumper Stickers Against
Any and Everybody

Help Us Keep America Gay
Support Your Local KKK

COMMUNISTS FONDLE SOFA CREVICES

May Your Soul Be Forever Tormented
By FIRE And Your Bones Dug Up
By Dogs and Dragged Through the
Streets of Minneapolis!!!

*subsidiary of K.K. Katzenberger Konglomerate, Inc.

NATHAN BEDFORD FORREST
WHITE BED SHEETS
MANUFACTURING COMPANY, INC.*

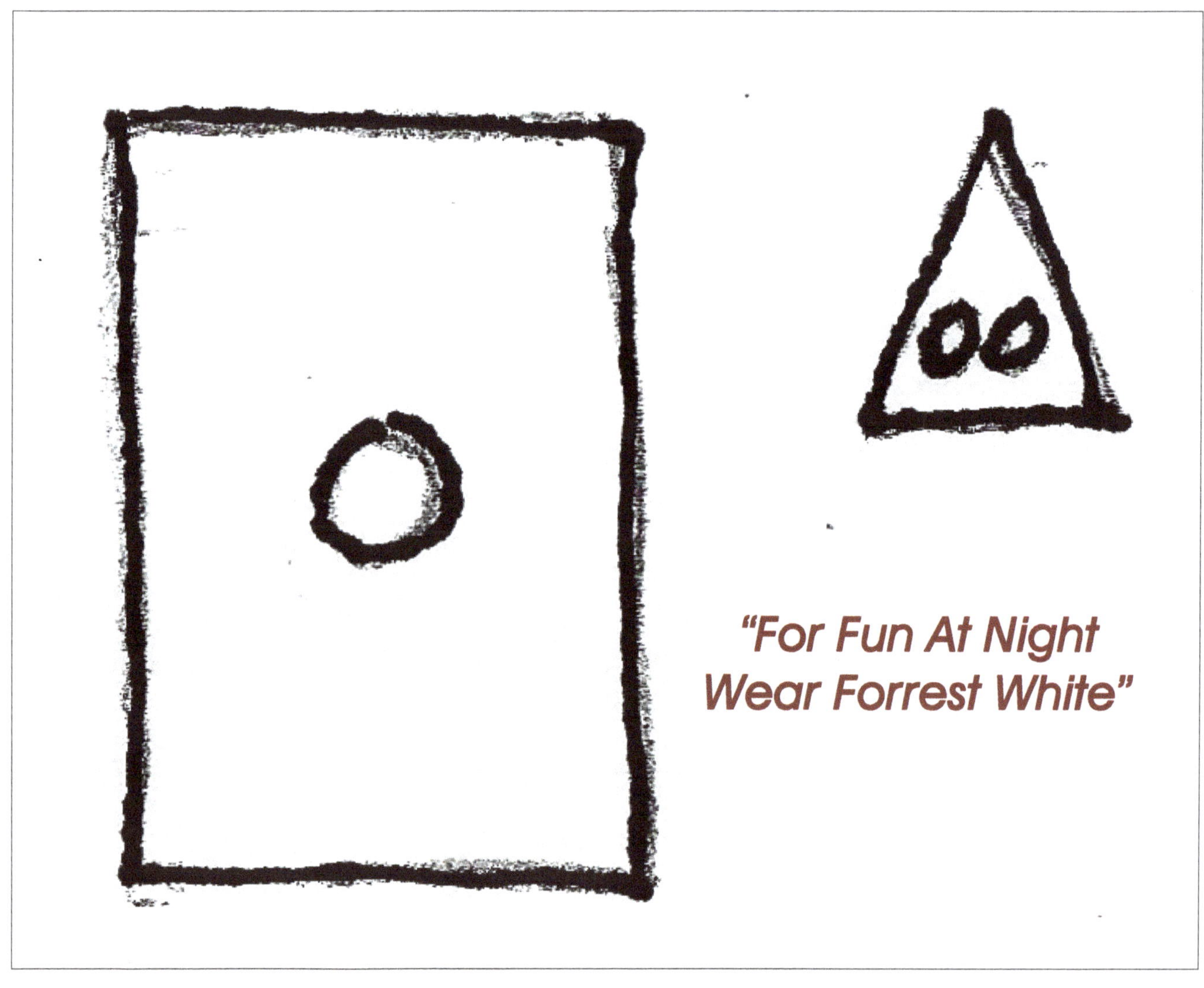

*subsidiary of K.K. Katzenberger Konglomerate, Inc.

PEEKY POO NUDIST KAMP, INC.*

HOODS AND ROBES BY KUTIES, INC.*

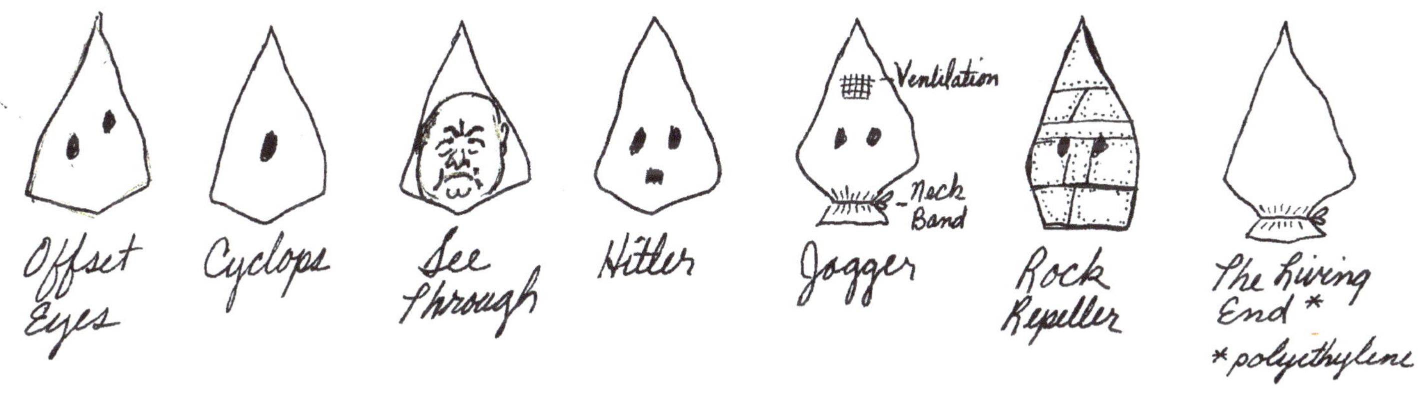

BO BO LEDBETTER'S LUMBER YARDS, INC.*

"For A Better Built Cross Use Bo Bo's Wood"

*subsidiary of K.K. Katzenberger Konglomerate, Inc.

GLOSSARY OF KLAN TERMINOLOGY

AKIA a password meaning "A Klansman I Am;" often seen on decals and bumper stickers. These are also the initials for Amalgamated Katzenbergr Industrial Associates of which Nathan Bedford Forrest White Bed Sheets Manufacturing Company, Inc. is a subsidiary.

AYAK? a password meaning "Are You A Klansman?" This is also the Tibetian response to the frequently asked tourist question "What's 'at big 'ole, hairy thang over 'ere 'at sorta looks like a cow?"

CA BARK a password meaning "Constantly Applied By All Real Klansmen." Do not confuse with CA MEOW which is the password for a secret old men's organization "Curmudgeons Advance for Men's Eminence Over Women!"

Exalted Cyclops* the top officer, or president, of a klavern, usually referred to as the "E.C." Originated with "General Faubus Bullthropp who was born with only one eye, smack dab in the middle of his forehead.

Genii* the collective name for the national officers who serve as an advisory board to the Imperial Wizard. Genii is a pluralization of genius meaning an attendant spirit or person who influences another person. Unkind critics are prone to point out that the title has nothing to do with the more common usage of "genius," for intelligence or wisdom.

Ghouls	term for rank and file Klansmen, though seldom used because of its ugly associations with grave robbing and corpse eating.
Grand Dragon*	the top officer of a Realm, or state president. Old "Triple K's" perverted sense of humor shines through here with his origination of the title "Dragon." His familiarity with the origins of ancient words led him to use this derivative of the Greek work *drakon* which came from a remote verb meaning "to look at" and "to flash." Until it was removed as a part of the swearing-in ceremony, after "Triple K's" death, new Grand Dragons were required "to flash" themselves before the entire assembly.
Grand Wizard*	the title conferred on Nathan Bedford Forest, head of the Reconstruction Klan comparable to the Imperial Wizard. While Ku Kluxers are not noted for their humor, they dearly love such double entendres as: *"'at 'ole Bubba Shrum certainly is a grand wizard unduh the sheet!"*
Imperial Klonvo- kation	national convention, usually held biennially. Rather than being housed in big hotels and convention halls like those of Republicans and Democrats, the Klan rotates its conventions across the country, using one of the many Katzenberger warehouses.
Imperial Tax	a percentage of the dues sent to national headquarters. The same as with federal land and state taxes, the Klan's Imperial Tax goes for such worthwhile causes as salaries for dedicated and selfless officials. While these men love their country, they expect to be paid for it.
Imperial Wizard*	the overall, or national, head of a Klan, who is sometimes compared to the President of the United States. As with all politicians he is a man of great purity of purpose, intelligence,

compassion, depth of philosophical understanding, and honor. He is a major recipient of the Imperial Tax.

Inner Circle
small group of four or five members who plan and carry out "action" such as cross burnings, bullying, harassment, and general mayhem in order to promote Americanism and Christianity, and thereby turn other from their evil ways.

Invisible Empire
a Ku Klux Klan's overall jurisdiction, which it compares to the United States, although none exist in some states. The Klan doesn't favor one region of America over another. It will come in and set up house wherever good people will allow it.

K
symbol for potassium.

K. K.
as with all organizations there are those who are an embarrassment to the general membership. In the Klan it is the Klan Kuties, a group of preverts who wear nothing under their unofficial, garishly colored robes and use "see-through" hoods thereby displaying their gold earrings, eye makeup, beauty spots, and "stylish" hairdos.

K. K. K.
initials of "Triple K's" grandson and present board chairman of Nathan Bedford Forrest White Bed Sheets Manufacturing Company, Inc., "Knock Kneed" Katzenberger III.

Ka Ka
the words used by Klan parents when teaching their children bowel control as in, *"Does Baby Sister need to go sit on the potty to make Ka Ka?"*

Kalendar
Klan calendar, which dates events from both its origin and 1915 rebirth. "Anno Klan" means in the year of the Klan. The months are called Bloody, Gloomy, Hideous, Fearful, Furious, Alarming, Terrible, Horrible, Mournful, Sorrowful, Frightful, and Appalling. The weeks are Woeful, Weeping, Wailing, Wonderful, and Weird, and the days are Dar, deadly, Dismal,

Doleful, Desolate, Dreadful, and Desperate. Whoever said the Klan doesn't have a sense of humor?

Kangaroo a herbivorous, leaping marsupial, boxing mammal found in Australia and New Guinea. On October 5, 1936, the kangaroo was adopted as the Klan's official animal.

Kardinal Kullors white, crimson, gold, and black. Secondary Kullors are gray, green, and blue. The Imperial Wizzard's Kullor is "royal" purple. Even the Klan has been influenced by America's sexual revolution as seen in the outrageous pastel combinations used on robes and "see through" hoods worn by a kinky group who refer to themselves as Klan Kuties.

KBI Klan Bureau of Investigation. Standards for selection into the KBI are extremely high. They require the ability:
- to find one's own naval
- to isochronically pat one's head and rub one's stomach
- to differentiate between black and white.

KIGY "Klansman, I Greet You!" Should not be confused when seen on Iowa license plates where it stands for Kalispell Idahoans Grow Yams.

Kiwi a flightless New Zealand bird.

Klavern a local unit or club, also called a "den." There are also Klan Youth Corps which are compared to the Cub Scouts and Brownies thereby evidencing the Klan's contribution to the American way of life.

Klectokon initiation fees and dues. Some bad-tempered Ku Kluxers denounce the Klectokon and Imperial Tax as nothing more than legalized kleptomania.

Klodes	songs sung at Klonvocations. A good example is the ever popular "The Ku Klux Klan, White Man's Burden Blues."
Klokard	lecturer and teacher of Klancraft (the Klan's practices and beliefs. Foremost among many men of brilliance was Great Klokard Earl Dee Brightwater who believed that *"until you have walked a mile in another man's rubber boots you can't imagine the smell."*
Kloran	Klan Bible. The Kloran makes clear much that is theologically confusing by explaining what GOD was *really* thinking and what HE *really* meant when HE dictated THE BIBLE.
Kludd	Klan chaplain. These wonderful men are noted for their possession of truth and willingness to burn you at the stake if you disagree with them.
Klutz	a dumb Klansman who is prone to run into thee sides of doorways, and is usually given the task of lighting the cross.
Knight-Hawks*	custodian of the fiery cross and of applicants immediately prior to their initiation, and in some Klans, responsible for carrying out violence. The office is often designated by a black robe. This is one of the Klan's toughest jobs. Knight-hawks find it next to impossible to get any form of insurance and when they do, the rates are exorbitant. Job stress results in a high rate of "burnout" and psychosis, in the form of pyromania, is not uncommon. These guys can really look and act scary, especially when they dress in all black and talk like Darth Vader.
Knockers	the mammary glands of Klanswomen.
Knurd	same as a Klutz.

Konx   sound made by a pebble falling into an ancient Elwsinion voting urn.

Kook   a mentally ill Klansman.

Kosher   good Jewish food.

Kraken   a Norwegian sea monster of great size.

Krap   KKK body waste production.

Kudos   the fame, glory and credit (plus money) which the author and artist hope to receive for creating this outstanding literary work.

Kultur   something most Klansmen ain't got.

The above officers exist on national, state, and province levels. Their titles are then prefaced by "Imperial" on the national level, "Grand" on the state level, and "Great" on the Province level.

APPLICATION FOR CITIZENSHIP

in the

Invisible Empire

Knights of the Ku Klux Klan

Incorporated

****

To His Majesty the Imperial Wizard, Emperor of the Invisible Empire, Knights of the Ku Klux Klan

I, the undersigned, a native born, true and loyal citizen of the United States of America, being a white male Gentile person of temperate habits, sound in mind and a believer in the tenants of the Christian religion, the maintenance of white supremacy and the principles of "pure Americanism," apply for membership in the Knights of the Ku Klux Klan through

Klan No. ...., Realm of ....

I guarantee on my honor to conform strictly to all rules and requirements regulating my "naturalization" and the continuance of my membership, and at all times a strict and loyal obedience to your constitutional authority and the constitution and laws of the fraternity, not in conflict with the constitution and constitutional laws of the United States of America and the states thereof. If I prove to be untrue as a Klansman I will willingly accept as my portion whatever penalty your authority may impose.

The required "klectoken" of $173.19 accompanies this application

Signed..............................…..................Applicant

Endorsed by

KI...Residence Address...

KI...Business Address...

Date..Year.........